THE ZACK FILES

My
Teacher Ate My Homework

LETTERS TO DAN GREENBURG
ABOUT THE ZACK FILES:

From a mother in New York, NY: "Just wanted to let you know that it was THE ZACK FILES that made my son discover the joy of reading...I tried everything to get him interested...THE ZACK FILES turned my son into a reader overnight. Now he complains when he's out of books!"

From a boy named Toby in New York, NY: "The reason why I like your books is because you explain things that no other writer would even dream of explaining to kids."

From Tara in Floral Park, NY: "When I read your books I felt like I was in the book with you. We love your books!"

From a teacher in West Chester, PA: "I cannot thank you enough for writing such a fantastic series."

From Max in Old Bridge, NJ: "I wasn't such a great reader until I discovered your books."

From Monica in Burbank, IL: "I read almost all of your books and I loved the ones I read. I'm a big fan! *I'm Out of My Body, Please Leave a Message*. That's a funny title. It makes me think of it being the best book in the world."

From three mothers in Toronto: "You have managed to take three boys and unlock the world of reading. In January they could best be characterized as boys who 'read only under duress.' Now these same guys are similar in that they are motivated to READ."

From Stephanie in Hastings, NY: "If someone didn't like your books that would be crazy."

From Dana in Floral Park, NY: "I really LOVE I mean LOVE your books. I read them a million times. I wish I could buy more. They are so good and so funny."

From a teacher in Pelham, NH: "My students are thoroughly enjoying [THE ZACK FILES]. Some are reading a book a night."

From Madeleine in Hastings, NY: "I love your books...I hope you keep making many more Zack Files."

THE ZACK FILES™

My Teacher Ate My Homework

By Dan Greenburg

Illustrated by Jack E. Davis

GROSSET & DUNLAP • NEW YORK

For Judith, and for the real Zack,
with love—D.G.

I'd like to thank my editor
Jane O'Connor, who makes the process
of writing and revising so much fun,
and without whom
these books would not exist.

I also want to thank
Emily Sollinger and Megan Bryant
for their terrific ideas.

Text copyright © 2002 by Dan Greenburg. Illustrations copyright © 2002 by Jack E. Davis.
All rights reserved. Published by Grosset & Dunlap, a division of Penguin Putnam Books
for Young Readers, 345 Hudson Street, New York, NY 10014. GROSSET & DUNLAP and
THE ZACK FILES are trademarks of Penguin Putnam Inc. Published simultaneously in
Canada. Printed in the U.S.A.

Library of Congress Cataloging-in-Publication Data

Greenburg, Dan.
    My teacher ate my homework / by Dan Greenburg ; illustrated by Jack E. Davis.
      p. cm. — (Zack files ; 27)
    Summary: After she eats his homework, ten-year-old Zack suspects that his substitute
teacher Mrs. Wolfowitz is a werewolf and uncovers her bizarre secret.
    [1. Werewolves—Fiction. 2. Substitute teachers—Fiction. 3. Teachers—Fiction.
4. Schools—Fiction. 5. Humorous stories.] I. Davis, Jack E., ill. II. Title. III. Series:
Greenburg, Dan. Zack files ; v 27.
PZ7.G8278 Myf 2002
[Fic]—dc21

                                                 2002007510

ISBN 0-448-42683-8   A B C D E F G H I J

Chapter 1

I know that substitute teachers have a tough job. But does that give one the right to bite me on the butt?

I guess maybe I'm getting ahead of myself.

My name is Zack. I'm ten-and-a-half, and I'm in the fifth grade at the Horace Hyde-White School for Boys. That's in New York City, by the way. My parents are divorced, and I spend about half my time with my dad. It's when I'm with my dad that the weird things happen. Like this time I started telling you about.

My regular science and homeroom teacher, Mrs. Coleman-Levin, was out sick. Instead, we had a substitute teacher, Mrs. Wolfowitz. As soon as I saw her, I thought there was something strange about her. She was short, dark and very hairy. There seemed to be stubble on her cheeks from shaving, but it was also on her nose and forehead. She didn't stand upright. She sort of crouched over. And when I turned in my science homework...Well, I can't be sure of this, but I thought I heard her growl.

"Excuse me, ma'am," I said. "Did you just growl?"

She gave me an angry look. It was the wrong thing to say. I realized that as soon as I said it.

"What is your name, young man?" she asked.

"Uh, it's Zack."

"Well, Zack," she said, "I was most certainly not growling. I was clearing my throat. And I'd like to see you after class."

Uh-oh. Well, that's what you get for asking a teacher if she was growling.

OK, what's the worst she could do to me? Kick me out of class, just because I asked if she was growling? No way.

When science class was over and everybody filed out of the room, I walked up to the teacher's desk.

"Mrs. Wolfowitz," I said. "What did you want to see me about?"

Mrs. Wolfowitz glared at me over the top of her glasses. Then she yawned. While her mouth was open, I caught a peek at her teeth. They looked a little more fangy than toothy. I wondered whether I should mention it. I realized it would probably be another bad mistake. "Why, Mrs. Wolfowitz, what big teeth you have!" would definitely be the wrong thing to say at this point.

"Did you hand in your homework?" asked Mrs. Wolfowitz.

"Yes, ma'am," I said. "I handed it in before class."

"Then where is it?"

I pointed at my homework. It was lying on her desk right in front of her.

"Right there," I said.

"Right where?" she said.

"Right there. See?" I pointed again.

She bent low over my homework. Then she did something very weird. She licked it. I decided to pretend I hadn't seen her do that.

Then she did something even weirder.

~ 4 ~

She opened her mouth, grabbed my homework in her enormous teeth, and began chewing it up.

I watched her eat my homework without saying anything. What could I say? I was scared to mention what she was doing, but I was also scared not to. Soon, she'd pretty much eaten the whole thing. Finally, I couldn't stand it any longer.

"Excuse me, ma'am," I said. "But why did you do that?"

"Why did I do what?" she asked.

"Eat my homework."

"Don't be ridiculous," she said. "Why would I eat your homework?"

"Are you denying you ate it?" I asked.

"Absolutely," she said. "And I'll thank you not to make such insulting accusations again. I happen to be a highly respected substitute teacher. In fact, I've received awards for my substitute teaching. Schools

actually hope their regular teachers will get sick, just so I can substitute for them."

I knew I should let it go, but I just couldn't.

"Mrs. Wolfowitz, if you didn't eat my homework, then where is it?"

Now she was really mad.

"You obviously failed to bring it in, didn't you?" she said.

"Mrs. Wolfowitz," I said quietly, "you know that isn't true."

"Are you calling me a liar?" she asked.

"No, ma'am. I'm just saying I brought my homework in and you ate it. Look. There's a tiny piece of it still stuck in the corner of your mouth. See?"

I reached up to get it. Mrs. Wolfowitz almost bit my finger off.

I ran out of there before she could find any more parts of me to taste.

Chapter 2

"Yes, Zack, what is it?" said Mr. Underpence.

He's the new principal of my school. I had gone to see him right after Mrs. Wolfowitz nearly bit my finger off.

"Sir, I'm having kind of a problem with my substitute teacher."

"Mrs. Wolfowitz?"

"Yes, sir," I said.

"Fine woman, Mrs. Wolfowitz. Fine woman," said Mr. Underpence. "Won awards for her substitute teaching, I hear. We'd been *hoping* one of our teachers would get sick so she could substitute here. And Mrs. Coleman-Levin was good enough to oblige us. What sort of problem are you having with Mrs. Wolfowitz?"

"Well, sir, she kind of ate my homework."

"Excuse me?"

"I said Mrs. Wolfowitz ate my homework."

Mr. Underpence frowned.

"That's preposterous," he said. "Why on earth would Mrs. Wolfowitz eat your homework?"

"I have no idea," I said. "All I know is that she did."

"Well, that's poppycock," said Mr. Underpence. "Sheer poppycock. Zack, I'm very disappointed in you. Coming in here and telling me such poppycock. I'd like your father to come to my office for a conference tomorrow."

"But, sir..."

Mr. Underpence checked his schedule.

"Eight a.m. I'd like to see you both."

Oh boy. Now I was really in trouble. I was pretty sure Dad would believe that Mrs. Wolfowitz ate my homework. Still, he was going to be mad at me for making him give up valuable work time to come to school.

At lunch, I told my friend Spencer everything that had happened. We were moving down the cafeteria line with our trays. I told him about how Mrs. Wolfowitz ate my homework. "She scares me," I said. "I mean, she has these sharp fangs and she growls. And isn't she awfully hairy for a lady?"

Spencer nodded. Then he checked his watch. It's a cool one that tells you the date, the phases of the moon and stuff like that.

"You know, there's a full moon tomorrow night," said Spencer.

"So?" I said, moving down to desserts. I grabbed a slice of banana cream pie.

"So think what you just told me about Mrs. Wolfowitz," said Spencer. "Mrs. *Wolf*owitz. Aren't you beginning to suspect she might be a..."

"—werewolf?" I finished Spencer's sentence.

Spencer nodded. He didn't act like this was some terrible problem. He acted like I'd given him this huge gift.

"Zack, this is so cool!" said Spencer.

"What's so cool about it?" I asked.

I paid for my lunch and started looking around for a place to sit.

"Well, we can follow her around with my camcorder and catch her doing something wolfy," said Spencer. "Then, when Mrs.

Coleman-Levin gets back, we turn in the tape for an extra-credit science project. Do you realize how great that would be? A videotape of a real werewolf? We'll probably both get A-pluses!"

"Whoa," I said. "Hang on a second. All I said was that Mrs. Wolfowitz ate my homework, that's all. And that she's kind of strange looking."

"Zack," said Spencer, "how well do I know you?"

"As well as anybody, I guess."

We sat down.

"And you mean to tell me you don't think she's a werewolf?" said Spencer.

"*Who's* a werewolf?" said a voice at the table just behind us.

I turned around. It was Vernon. Vernon Manteuffel, the rich kid in our class who sweats a lot. He's the biggest blabbermouth in school, and he's always trying to get me in trouble. His tray was loaded with food, mostly desserts.

"Nobody's a werewolf, Manteuffel," I said.

"Nobody?" Vernon repeated. "But I distinctly heard you say that Mrs. Wolfowitz ate your homework. And I distinctly heard Spencer say that she was a werewolf."

"If you distinctly heard us say that," I said, "then why did you ask?"

"I wanted to be sure," said Vernon. "Boy, wait till I tell the kids in class that our substitute teacher is a werewolf!"

"Uh, please don't do that, Vernon," I said.

"Why not?" he asked.

"Because you wouldn't want to get an innocent woman in trouble."

"She doesn't sound so innocent to *me,*" said Vernon. "What did you do when she ate your homework?"

"Look," I said, "I really don't want this to go any further. If I tell you what happened, will you promise not to tell anybody else?"

"On my word of honor," said Vernon.

On his word of honor. That was a laugh, the idea that Vernon Manteuffel had any honor. It was probably a stupid idea to trust him to do anything, but I never seem to learn. So I told him everything that happened. And, in front of me and Spencer, he swore on his word of honor that he wouldn't tell.

Well, if he did, I'd tell everybody Vernon was a bedwetter.

Chapter 3

That night, I told my dad what happened to my homework. Dad is great. He always understands whatever I tell him.

"I don't understand, Zack," said Dad. "You think your teacher is a werewolf just because she ate your homework? Maybe she just likes to eat paper. Some people do."

"I never heard of anybody who liked to eat paper," I said.

"Really?" said Dad. "I've been known to nibble paper myself. Especially if I'm writing an article and it isn't going too well. It's kind of a nervous habit. I just don't see why eating your homework makes her a werewolf."

"Well, that wasn't the only thing," I said. "Also, she's very dark and very hairy. You know the stubble you get on your cheeks after you shave your beard? Well, it's all over her face, even on her nose. And she doesn't stand up straight. She kind of crouches. And she has these really long teeth."

"I know lots of people who are dark and hairy, who don't stand up straight, and who have long teeth," said Dad. "But none of them is a werewolf. At least none of them has bitten me."

"The biting probably comes next," I said. "Anyway, Dad, it doesn't matter whether you believe she's a werewolf or not. What I'm trying to tell you is that the principal wants to see both of us in his office tomorrow morning. At eight a.m. sharp."

"Is Mrs. Wolfowitz going to be there, too?"

"I don't know. Why?"

"Well," said Dad, "if she is, maybe I can interview her. I've never done an interview with a werewolf before."

By the time we got to the principal's office the next morning, I was pretty nervous. I didn't know what the principal would do to me if we couldn't convince him I was telling the truth.

"Well well, thanks for coming, sir," said Mr. Underpence, shaking hands with Dad. "Sit down, sit down."

Dad and I both sat down opposite the principal.

"Good," said Mr. Underpence. "Now, Zack, tell us what happened."

"I already told you," I said. "Mrs. Wolfowitz ate my homework."

"Mmmm," said Mr. Underpence. "I see you haven't changed your story."

"Why should I change my story?" I said. "That's what happened."

The principal turned to Dad. "What do *you* say about this?" he asked.

"If Zack says his teacher ate his homework, then I believe him," said Dad.

The principal frowned. I think he'd tried so hard to get Mrs. Wolfowitz as a teacher, he now refused to hear anything bad about her. Would I have to say I made up the story about Mrs. Wolfowitz, so I wouldn't be suspended?

"Have you asked Mrs. Wolfowitz about this matter?" Dad asked.

"You mean, have I asked her whether she ate a student's homework?"

"Right," said Dad.

"Well, of course not," said Mr. Underpence. "That would be insulting."

"Don't you think it's insulting to Zack to believe he's lying to you?" Dad asked.

"But Zack is a *child*," said Mr. Underpence. "Mrs. Wolfowitz is an *adult*."

"So you automatically take an adult's side against a child's?" said Dad. "That doesn't sound as though you have a high opinion of children. Which would be a disappointing thing to see in a principal. I wonder what the school's board of directors would think about that."

A little vein stood out on the principal's forehead. It was throbbing.

"You know what I'm thinking?" said Mr. Underpence with a nasty smile.

"What?" said Dad.

"I'm thinking perhaps Zack ought to be

suspended for lying about a teacher. I shall notify you of my decision."

Then Mr. Underpence stood up. The meeting was obviously over.

Chapter 4

"**D**ad, you were fantastic!" I said as soon as we got out of the principal's office. "Thanks for sticking up for me. And if I get suspended, it was worth it."

"Oh, I don't think you'll get suspended," said Dad. "But I'd steer clear of Mrs. Wolfowitz today if I were you."

So Dad wrote me a note. I skipped both homeroom and science class that day. That afternoon during study hall, Spencer and I went to the library and did some research on werewolves. I tried to tell him about the meeting with Mr. Underpence, but the librarian kept shushing us.

We learned lots of cool stuff. Like: (1) You can become a werewolf if another werewolf bites you, or if somebody casts a spell on you, or if you're born to a werewolf mom. (2) Werewolves don't get sick or get old or die, but you can kill them if you get them in the heart or the brain. (3) People who become werewolves can be cured, unless they taste human blood or flesh first. (Yuck!) (4) Werewolves mostly change into wolf form during the full moon. And Spencer was right. Tonight there was going to be a full moon.

After school, Spencer and I waited in the bushes till Mrs. Wolfowitz came out. Spencer had gotten his camcorder out of his locker and was putting in a new cassette.

While we waited, I told him what Dad said in the principal's office. He was pretty impressed.

"Your dad really has a lot of guts to threaten old Underpence," said Spencer.

"I don't really think he was threatening him," I said.

"You don't?"

"Well, maybe he was," I said. "You think Underpence is going to suspend me?"

"Oh, almost certainly," said Spencer.

"Are you serious?" I said. "Spencer, what'll I do if he suspends me?"

Spencer shrugged. "Go to another school, I guess," he said.

We waited and waited. Mrs. Wolfowitz didn't come out.

"Why isn't she coming out?" I asked.

"I don't know," said Spencer. "Maybe she left by the back entrance."

"Why would she do that?" I asked.

"Or maybe..."

"Yes?"

"Maybe she's waiting till it gets dark," said Spencer.

Maybe Spencer was right. Werewolves don't like sunlight. Maybe Mrs. Wolfowitz was afraid of the sunlight. Maybe she really *was* a werewolf. The thought gave me the creeps.

We continued to wait. After a while, the sun set and it started to get dark.

"This is silly," I said. "She's already left by the back entrance. We're standing here for nothing."

"You want to leave?" Spencer asked. "What if she comes out right after we leave?"

"She's not here anymore," I said. "I'm getting cold. I think we should go home."

"Whatever you say," said Spencer.

He started packing up his camcorder.

Just then, the front door of the school opened.

"Look!" I whispered.

It was Mrs. Wolfowitz! She looked around nervously, then she walked down the steps to the sidewalk. Spencer and I crouched lower in the bushes.

"And you wanted to leave," Spencer whispered.

"Oh, shut up," I whispered.

Mrs. Wolfowitz started down the street. We let her get half a block ahead of us, then we started to follow.

"You think she's going home?" I said.

"How should I know?" said Spencer.

A sudden ice-cold wind came up and blew dead leaves in my face. I shivered and brushed them away. The sun had set already, but it wasn't very dark out. I looked up at the sky and realized why. It was a full moon, just as Spencer said.

Mrs. Wolfowitz walked along the street for several blocks in that strange hunched-over walk of hers. We followed, trying to keep out of sight. Then Mrs. Wolfowitz turned into an alley.

"Why in the world is she going down that alley?" I whispered.

"I don't know," said Spencer. "Maybe she lives there. Let's follow."

We waited about thirty seconds. Then we followed. When we got to the corner, we peeked down the alley. By the light of the full moon we saw an incredible sight. In back of a butcher shop, Mrs. Wolfowitz had turned over a big plastic garbage can. She was digging in the garbage. After a while she found what looked like a huge bone.

"Spencer," I whispered. "Shoot this!"

We crept forward and hid behind another garbage can. Spencer took out his camcorder and began to shoot.

Mrs. Wolfowitz held the bone in both paws—I mean hands—and began to gnaw on it.

"Do you believe this?" I whispered.

Spencer giggled.

"Yuck!" I whispered. "Can you imagine what that old bone tastes like?"

"No," Spencer whispered, "but I can practically taste that A-plus this tape is going to get us."

Mrs. Wolfowitz stopped chewing and looked around nervously. Maybe she heard us whispering. We ducked down behind the garbage can. After a minute or so, we peeked out. She was gone!

"Oh, no," I said. "We've lost her!"

"No you haven't," said a voice behind us.

I turned around.

It was Mrs. Wolfowitz!

Chapter 5

Mrs. Wolfowitz had a crazy smile on her face. Her eyes were practically popping out of her head. I was so scared, I was afraid I'd pee in my pants.

"What are you doing here?" she asked. "Are you spying on me?"

"S-s-spying?" I repeated. "N-n-no, of course not, Mrs. W-wolfowitz."

"Then why is Spencer holding that camcorder?" she asked.

"Which camcorder?" I said.

She pointed.

"*That* camcorder," she said.

"Oh, *th-that* camcorder," I said.

"Yes, *that* camcorder," said Mrs. Wolfowitz.

"W-well, there's a very simple explanation for that," said Spencer.

"And what is it?" said Mrs. Wolfowitz.

"W-we're making a d-documentary," said Spencer. "On alleys."

"Is that so?" said Mrs. Wolfowitz.

"Th-that happens to be the honest t-truth," said Spencer.

"Do you know what Mr. Underpence told me this afternoon?" said Mrs. Wolfowitz. "He said Vernon Manteuffel told him that Zack thinks I'm a werewolf."

"A w-werewolf?" I repeated. "Th-that's ridiculous, ma'am! You? A werewolf?" I burst into hysterical laughter.

Suddenly Mrs. Wolfowitz growled a terrible growl. She lunged straight at me.

I side-stepped her. She tripped and fell. "Run, Spencer, run!" I shouted.

I ran. Spencer followed. We raced down the alley as fast as we could go. Mrs. Wolfowitz loped after us, growling louder than ever.

When we got to the end of the alley, we turned left onto the street and ran back in the direction of school. It was brighter on the street than in the alley. I prayed somebody would see us and save us.

Running for his life, Spencer pulled ahead of me. We were running so fast, it was hard to breathe. My heart was pounding away in my chest. My lungs were practically bursting. I looked back. Mrs. Wolfowitz was gaining on us!

Up ahead, a man in a tuxedo was walking his dog. The dog saw us and growled. Behind us, Mrs. Wolfowitz growled at the dog.

"Help us!" I shouted ahead to the man in the tuxedo. "We're being chased by a werewolf!"

"My word!" said the man in the tuxedo. He had a British accent. "How do you know she's a werewolf?"

"She ate my homework!" I shouted as I caught up to him.

"That doesn't prove she's a werewolf," said the man in the tuxedo. "Perhaps she just likes to eat paper. I confess that—"

"Never mind," I said as I ran past him. Talking was using up breath I needed for running.

"—I eat paper myself," called the man in the tuxedo, running after me. "It's quite tasty, really. I don't see how eating your homework makes her a werewolf. Do you have any *proof* she's a werewolf?"

"Just forget it, OK?" I gasped.

We must have been a weird-looking group, running down the street. First came Spencer with his camcorder. Right behind Spencer was me. Behind me was the man in the tuxedo leading his dog. And behind the dog was Mrs. Wolfowitz.

"I'm quite serious, actually," called the man in the tuxedo. "Deciding this woman is a werewolf without proof is terribly unfair."

"I said forget it!" I shouted. I looked back. Mrs. Wolfowitz was gaining on me. Now she was almost up to the man in the tuxedo.

"I couldn't help overhearing," called Mrs. Wolfowitz. "Thanks for seeing my side of it."

"You're quite welcome," puffed the man in the tuxedo. "It's the only civilized thing to do."

 35

"Oh, I quite agree," said Mrs. Wolfowitz. "Seeing both sides is the only civilized way."

Then Mrs. Wolfowitz sprang at me and bit a big hole in the seat of my pants.

Chapter 6

We ran for a few more blocks, then we lost Mrs. Wolfowitz.

Spencer and I were completely out of breath. It was cold out, but I was really sweating under my clothes.

"Boy...that was a close one," gasped Spencer.

"It...sure was," I said.

We were still puffing so hard, we could barely talk. Sweat was streaming down my face. My heart was beating like crazy.

"You know," I said, "Mrs. Coleman-

Levin...lives only a...few blocks from here. I really think...we need...her help."

"Good...idea," said Spencer.

I stopped at a pay phone to call Dad. I was afraid he might be worrying where I was.

"Zack," said Dad when he answered the phone. "Where have you been? I was worried about you."

"I'm...fine," I said. "I'm...with Spencer. We're...doing an extra-credit...science project...for school."

"Why are you so out of breath?"

"Well...we were running," I said.

"Say, you aren't in any trouble, are you?"

"No," I said.

"Does this have anything to do with Mrs. Wolfowitz?" Dad asked.

"Maybe...a little bit," I said. "We're going over to...Mrs. Coleman-Levin's place now. I'll be...home soon."

I hung up the phone before he could tell me not to go.

A few minutes later, we buzzed Mrs. Coleman-Levin from the lobby of her building. She didn't buzz back. She got on the intercom instead.

"Who's there?" she asked.

"It's Zack and Spencer," I said.

"Zack and Spencer," she repeated. "What are you boys doing here?"

"Oh," I said. "Well, we're having kind of a problem, and we thought you could help us."

"I'm afraid this isn't a good time for me," she said.

"Why not?" I said. "Are you sick, Mrs. Coleman-Levin?"

"Not sick, Zack. Just a bit hazy."

"Mrs. Coleman-Levin, this is really important. If you can possibly let us come up and talk to you, it would really help."

I could hear her sigh over the intercom.

"Very well," she said. "Come on up. But I told you, I'm a bit hazy."

We went up in the elevator. When she finally opened her door, it was a little hard to see her. Not because it was dark in her apartment, although it *was* dark in her apartment. It was because Mrs. Coleman-Levin was really hazy. I could sort of see right through her. There were tons of palm trees in her apartment and a little waterfall. There was something burning. It smelled OK, though. I remembered what it was. Incense.

"So, boys," said Mrs. Coleman-Levin, "what can I do for you?"

"Our new substitute teacher, Mrs. Wolfowitz, is acting really weird," I said.

"Weird? In what way?"

"Well, yesterday she ate my homework," I said. "And tonight she bit a hole in the seat of my pants."

"Well, she must have had a perfectly good reason," said Mrs. Coleman-Levin.

"What reason could she possibly have for eating my homework and biting a hole in the seat of my pants?"

I showed her the hole in my pants.

"Zack, that's embarrassing," said Mrs. Coleman-Levin. "Please sew up that hole as soon as you get home."

"OK," I said.

"Mrs. Coleman-Levin," said Spencer, "we're pretty sure Mrs. Wolfowitz is a werewolf."

"A werewolf?" said Mrs. Coleman-Levin. "Hmmm. Well, that's not surprising. I *thought* I'd noticed something odd about the woman. But somehow, the possibility she was a werewolf never entered my mind. I don't know why not."

Mrs. Coleman-Levin saw how sweaty we were. She insisted we go into her bathroom and wash up. When we came back into the living room, strange music was playing. I forget what they call the instrument, but I know it comes from India. And she had made us some kind of weird tea. It tasted like flowers. I didn't like it too much, but I didn't want to hurt her feelings.

"How is your tea?" asked Mrs. Coleman-Levin.

"Good," I said.

"Is this Lap-Sang Soo-Chong?" asked Spencer. Spencer knows everything.

"I'm afraid I can't tell you that," said Mrs. Coleman-Levin. "All right, boys, this is what I've decided we must do. First, I shall phone Mrs. Wolfowitz at home and convince her to come over here."

"You want her to come *here*?" I said. Seeing Mrs. Wolfowitz again tonight was about the last thing I wanted to do.

"Excuse me, Mrs. Coleman-Levin," said Spencer, "but that doesn't sound like such a great idea."

"Why not?" said Mrs. Coleman-Levin.

"Mrs. Wolfowitz is scary," I said. "I mean, she bites."

"Don't worry," said Mrs. Coleman-Levin, "I have a plan. We'll overpower her as soon as she comes in. Then we'll do something that will make it impossible for her to bite us."

"What are we going to do?" Spencer asked.

"I'd rather not tell you too much about it," she answered. "But it involves sprinkling powdered garlic, wolfsbane, deadly nightshade and catnip."

I didn't see how sprinkling powdered garlic, wolfsbane, deadly nightshade and catnip was going to protect us. But when it comes to stuff like substitute teachers who are werewolves, Mrs. Coleman-Levin is definitely the expert.

She gave Mrs. Wolfowitz time to get home, then she phoned her. She told Mrs. Wolfowitz she had to see her immediately to discuss tomorrow's lesson plan. Mrs. Wolfowitz didn't seem too anxious to come over. But nobody I know has ever been able to say no to Mrs. Coleman-Levin. She said she'd be over in about ten minutes.

I was pretty nervous about seeing her again, but Mrs. Coleman-Levin put us right to work getting ready.

Ten minutes later, Mrs. Wolfowitz was knocking on Mrs. Coleman-Levin's door. We were ready for her. Mrs. Coleman-Levin found an old hammock made of rope. We rigged it over the door. Spencer and I hid on both sides of the door. Each of us held on to one end of the hammock.

Mrs. Coleman-Levin had mixed up a cup full of garlic, wolfsbane, deadly nightshade and catnip.

Mrs. Coleman-Levin opened the door. Mrs. Wolfowitz was looking a lot wolfier. Plus she was drooling. Mrs. Coleman-Levin threw the stuff from the cup in Mrs. Wolfowitz's face. At the same time, Spencer and I tugged on both ends of the hammock. It fell right on top of her.

"W-what th—?" said Mrs. Wolfowitz.

"Pull!" yelled Spencer.

Spencer and I pulled tight on the ends of the hammock. Mrs. Wolfowitz was caught like an animal in a net. The stuff Mrs. Coleman-Levin threw in her face must have been pretty strong, because Mrs. Wolfowitz stopped struggling. She looked kind of sleepy.

"W-what are you doing to me?" she asked.

"Trying to help you," said Mrs. Coleman-Levin.

She raised both her hands over Mrs. Wolfowitz and began chanting in a spooky voice:

"Double Bubble, werewolf trouble,

Fangs and claws and shaving stubble."

There was a flash of blue light, and somewhere I heard the sound of thunder. Mrs. Coleman-Levin continued in her spooky voice:

"Horrid creature of the night,

I command you not to bite,

Not to snarl or growl or snap,

Just to take a teensy nap.

When you wake, you won't be bushy,

You'll have cheeks like a baby's tushy.

You won't be a wild creature,

Just a normal substitute teacher."

There was another flash of blue light and more thunder.

Mrs. Wolfowitz shook her head. "You don't understand," she said. "You've got it all wrong."

She looked pretty dazed. And I noticed she was changing. Her face was getting hairier. And her teeth were definitely turning into fangs.

"Really," said Mrs. Coleman-Levin. "Are you denying that a creature of the night bit you and transformed you into something hideous?"

"No no," she said, "that's just what happened. But I'm not a teacher who was bitten by a wolf. I'm a *wolf* who was bitten by a *teacher*."

"Hey, come on," said Spencer.

"I swear," said Mrs. Wolfowitz. "One night I'm in Yonkers with my husband and cubs. We're in a very woodsy section near the Saw Mill Parkway. We're minding our own business, pawing through some garbage cans in back of a house. It's a full moon. We hear this peculiar noise. Along comes a pack of teachers, looking for trouble. My husband and cubs got away. I wasn't so lucky. I got bitten."

"You got bitten by a teacher?" said Spencer.

"Just a flesh wound," she said. "It hardly broke the skin."

"And then what?" I said. "You started turning into a teacher?"

"Not at first," said Mrs. Wolfowitz. "At first I thought I was OK. I went back to my den, licked my wounds and went to sleep. The next morning at breakfast, my cubs were fighting over some papers we found in a garbage can. The papers had been used to wrap meat from the butcher shop, so they were a little bloody. I actually heard myself say, 'Eyes on our own papers, please.' My oldest wanted to go to the bathroom. I

~ 49 ~

heard myself say, 'Can't you wait till recess?' "

"Far out," said Spencer.

"Remarkable," said Mrs. Coleman-Levin.

"The next day," said Mrs. Wolfowitz, "I suddenly started walking on my hind legs. The day after that, I found myself at the mall, buying a dress and sensible shoes. It was pretty scary, I don't have to tell you."

"What did you do then?" I asked.

"What *could* I do?" she said. "I went into New York and joined the Teachers Union. The rest is history. I couldn't get a permanent job, but I was a darn good substitute, if I do say so myself. Although, to tell you the truth, I think I was a better wolf. And I miss my husband and cubs. Say, is it hot in here, or is it just me?"

Under the hammock, Mrs. Wolfowitz took off her shoes. Her feet had turned to paws. Her legs weren't just hairy, they were furry.

"How come you ate my homework?" I said. "And bit a hole in the seat of my pants?"

"Because you can take a wolf out of the woods," she said, "but you just can't take the wolf out of the teacher."

Mrs. Wolfowitz was becoming wolfier by the second. She had pointy wolf ears and a bushy tail. A minute later, she was a total wolf.

"You've been transformed back to what you were before you were bitten," said Mrs. Coleman-Levin. "It seems my ceremony was successful. What would you like us to do with you now?"

Mrs. Wolfowitz's answer was kind of hard to understand. It was half talking and half growling.

"Excuse me?" said Mrs. Coleman-Levin.

"I said that I'd surrre like to see my family again," said Mrs. Wolfowitz.

Mrs. Coleman-Levin nodded. She went to the hall closet and came back with a dog collar and a leash. She pulled the hammock off Mrs. Wolfowitz, helped her out of her clothes, and attached the collar and leash.

"Now then, who wants to go to Yonkers?" asked Mrs. Coleman-Levin.

Mrs. Wolfowitz threw her head back and howled. It creeped me out at first, but then I realized it was a happy howl.

Mrs. Coleman-Levin, Spencer, and I took Mrs. Wolfowitz out of the apartment on a leash. Mrs. Coleman-Levin had a very cool old Jaguar sedan in the basement garage. We all drove out to Yonkers and turned Mrs. Wolfowitz loose in the woods. She was on all fours now. But just before we drove away, I saw her lift one paw and wave.

The next day, Mrs. Coleman-Levin was back in homeroom, looking not at all hazy.

Because Vernon broke his promise and told on me to Mr. Underpence, I told all the kids in my class that Vernon was a bedwetter. They said they already knew.

When homeroom was over, Mrs. Coleman-Levin handed me a note in a sealed envelope. It was from Mr. Underpence. It said: "After careful consideration, I have decided not to suspend you. But kindly see to it that this sort of thing does not happen again."

Mrs. Coleman-Levin called me and Spencer aside.

"I reviewed the videotape you gave me," she said. "I think you two boys have done some remarkable research."

"Thank you," I said.

"Thank you," said Spencer.

"I am willing to consider this an extra-credit science project," she said. "On one condition."

"What's that?" I said.

"That you never mention the videotape or the science project or the entire incident to anybody. Because if you do, the magic I did in my apartment might stop working. And then something like this could happen again. Only next time it will be worse. Much worse."

We agreed not to tell anyone and left the classroom.

So that's pretty much what happened.

I just had a terrible thought, though. I've just told *you* every-thing that happened. Does that mean this will all happen again, only much worse?

What else happens to Zack?

Find out in

Tell a Lie and Your

Butt Will Grow

"I'm telling the truth," said Andrew. "I swear."

"Prove it," I said. "Take a lie detector test."

"Fine," said Andrew. "Do you have a lie detector?"

"No," I said, "but my dad is writing a magazine article about cops now. He's working at a police station, and I think they have a polygraph there. Polygraph means lie detector, in case you didn't know."

"Everybody knows a polygraph is a lie detector," said Andrew. "I learned that when I was two."

"So if my dad can arrange it, you'd come to the police station and take a polygraph test?"

"Sure," said Andrew.

I was amazed he agreed. But with all those kids there, he could hardly refuse.

THE ZACK FILES™

OUT-OF-THIS-WORLD FAN CLUB!

Looking for even more info on all the strange, otherworldly happenings going on in *The Zack Files*? Get the inside scoop by becoming a member of *The Zack Files* Out-Of-This-World Fan Club! Just send in the form below and we'll send you your *Zack Files* Out-Of-This-World Fan Club kit including an official fan club membership card, a really cool *Zack Files* magnet, and a newsletter featuring excerpts from Zack's upcoming paranormal adventures, supernatural news from around the world, puzzles, and more! And as a member you'll continue to receive the newsletter six times a year! The best part is—it's all free!

✄ --

☐ Yes! I want to check out *The Zack Files*
Out-Of-This-World Fan Club!

name: _____ age: _____

address: _____

city/town: _____ state: ___ zip: _____

Send this form to: Penguin Putnam Books for
Young Readers
Mass Merchandise Marketing
Dept. ZACK
345 Hudson Street
New York, NY 10014